Her Halloween Heartthrob

A SMALL TOWN HOLIDAY SWEET ROMANCE

SWEPT AWAY IN BUTTERCUP BAY
BOOK THREE

MOLLY ARDEN

Molly Arden
SWEET SMALL TOWN ROMANCE

Contents

CHAPTER 1

Natalie

THE ROAD into Buttercup Bay winds like a ribbon through the mountains, flanked by towering pines and vibrant autumn leaves. As I navigate the final bend, the town comes into view, a patchwork of charming cottages and rustic storefronts nestled along the edge of a sparkling bay.

My heart beats a little too fast, a mix of anxiety and anticipation swirling in my chest. The crisp autumn air is the first thing I notice as I step out of the car, the scent of pine and distant wood smoke filling my lungs. It's refreshing, yet there's an unfamiliarity to it that sets me on edge.

I glance down at my outfit—sleek black heels, a tailored coat, and a pencil skirt. The sharp lines of my clothing feel out of place here, like a jagged shard in an otherwise peaceful landscape. My breath hitches as I close the car door, the metallic clang echoing in the quiet street. Buttercup Bay is nothing like the bustling city I've left behind, and the realization that I don't belong here pricks at my confidence.

The Buttercup Inn stands proudly at the corner of the main street, its whitewashed walls adorned with verdant ivy that creeps playfully up the sides and vibrant flower baskets that sway gently in the breeze. The place exudes a charm that beckons me to linger, to fully immerse myself in the warmth of its inviting atmosphere, yet there's a tightness in my chest that urges me to hurry along. As I cross the threshold, the innkeeper greets me with a broad, welcoming smile, and I'm instantly enveloped by the cozy warmth radiating from the inn. The air is thick with the enticing scents of cinnamon and freshly baked bread, wrapping around me like a soft blanket, and for a fleeting moment, I experience a flicker of comfort that feels almost foreign. But just as quickly as it arrives, that sense of solace slips away, leaving me with the nagging reminder of my disconnection from this idyllic place.

"Welcome to Buttercup Bay, dear. I'm Lily. You must be Ms. Dawson," the innkeeper says, her voice a gentle lilt that perfectly complements the warm and inviting atmosphere of the inn. She appears to be my age, with auburn hair pulled back in a neat bun that accentuates her delicate features. Her eyes, sparkling with kindness and genuine warmth, convey a sense of familiarity that puts me slightly at ease, even amidst the lingering tension in my chest.

"Yes, that's me," I reply, forcing a smile that feels more strained than genuine.

"Long drive, I imagine. Your room is ready, and I've put a pot of tea on. Take your time to settle in. We don't rush things here." She hands me the key, her fingers brushing mine in a gesture that feels oddly intimate.

"Thank you," I manage, my voice catching in my throat. The warmth in her gaze makes me want to relax, to breathe, but my thoughts are already racing ahead.

As I make my way to my room, I can't help but reflect on how I ended up here—hundreds of miles from home, in a town I've never heard of until a few days ago. My career in advertising has been my everything for so long. I fought tooth and nail to climb the ladder in an industry that thrives on competition and ruthless ambition. But my last campaign flopped spectacularly, and the memory of it lingers like a bad taste in my mouth.

Derek's voice echoes in my mind, sharp and cutting as ever. "Maybe you're not cut out for this, Natalie. Not everyone has what it takes." The words, spoken just before he walked out of my life, still sting. I've been driven by the need to prove him wrong, to prove everyone wrong, but lately, that drive feels hollow. The success I've chased for so long is starting to feel like a mirage—always just out of reach, never as satisfying as I hoped.

I set my suitcase down by the bed, the soft creak of the wooden floor underfoot grounding me for a moment, a small reminder of the familiar comforts of home. The room is simple and cozy—exactly what I'd expect from a place like this, with its quaint decor and warm lighting that invites relaxation. But as I look out the window at the town below, my gaze sweeping over the quiet streets and the distant hills, the growing emptiness in my chest tightens its grip, an unwelcome companion that shadows my every thought.

I need to make this work. This campaign has to succeed. My career, my sense of self—everything is riding on it. But as I think about what lies ahead, about the task I've been given, a knot of anxiety coils in my stomach.

LATER, I find myself wandering into the heart of Buttercup Bay, drawn by the scent of something sweet. The main street is alive with the colors of fall —pumpkins on every porch, garlands of leaves draped across doorways, and the faint sound of children's laughter in the distance. My heels click against the cobblestones, a stark contrast to the soft crunch of leaves underfoot. I can't help but feel out of place, like an imposter in a world that's too warm, too welcoming for someone like me.

The café at the end of the street catches my eye, its windows fogged with warmth. Inside, the atmosphere is exactly what I expected—cozy and inviting, with the comforting scent of baked goods and fresh coffee hanging in the air. I order a slice of pumpkin pie, unable to resist the charm of the place. The woman behind the counter, Maggie Johnson, serves me with a smile that reaches her eyes.

"You must be new in town," she says as she sets the plate in front of me.

I nod. "Just arrived today."

Maggie leans on the counter, her gaze curious but not intrusive. "Buttercup Bay's a special place. Takes a little getting used to, though. What brings you here?"

I hesitate, unsure how much to share. "Work, mostly. I'm here to organize a photoshoot at some reclusive mountain man's home."

Her expression shifts slightly, a flicker of something —concern, maybe?—crossing her face. "I see. You might hear some talk around town about Jack Wilder. He's the one whose land you'll need for the shoot, I reckon."

The name catches my attention. "Jack Wilder?"

Maggie nods, her smile fading just a touch. "He's not fond of outsiders, especially those who come with big ideas. Jack's a good man, but he's been through a lot. Keeps to himself up in the mountains."

Her words are a gentle warning, but there's a challenge in her eyes that makes my resolve harden.

I've dealt with difficult people before—I can handle this. "Thank you for the advice," I say, trying to sound more confident than I feel.

She slides the plate closer to me. "Enjoy your pie, dear. And good luck."

As I take a bite, the rich, spiced flavor floods my senses, momentarily distracting me from the unease churning in my chest. The pie, warm and comforting, offers a brief respite from the weight of my thoughts. Yet, Maggie's words linger in the back of my mind, intertwining with my own swirling doubts and insecurities. Jack Wilder sounds like the last person who'd be inclined to help with my ambitious project, but I find myself cornered by necessity. I have to convince him—my career, my future, depends on it. The stakes have never felt higher, and the thought propels me to steel my resolve.

As I leave the café, the resolve in my steps feels stronger. Buttercup Bay may be a world away from everything I know, but I'm here to succeed. I can't afford to let anything—or anyone—get in my way.

CHAPTER 2

Jack

THE MORNING AIR IS COOL, crisp against my skin as I stand at the edge of my property. The mountain breeze ruffles my hair, carrying with it the scent of pine and damp earth. It's a smell I've come to rely on, grounding me in the life I've built out here, away from the chaos that once consumed me. The world is still, the only sound the soft rustling of leaves and the distant call of a bird. This is where I find peace—in the solitude of the mountains, surrounded by nothing but nature and the steady rhythm of my own heartbeat.

My cabin stands behind me, nestled among towering pines that have stood here longer than I've been alive. The logs are weathered, like me, but solid. The cabin is simple, and functional—a place where I can be alone, where the memories of what I've been through can't reach me. It's my sanctuary, my fortress. I built it with my own hands, each swing of the hammer a step further away from the life I left behind.

I grip the handle of my axe, the rough wood familiar against my calloused palms. There's a comfort in the weight of it, in the way it fits so naturally in my hands. Splitting wood has become a ritual for me—a way to clear my mind, to focus on something tangible, something I can control. I lift the axe and bring it down with practiced precision, the blade sinking into the log with a satisfying crack. The sound echoes in the stillness, a reminder that out here, I'm in control. Out here, I'm safe.

But even as I lose myself in the rhythm of the work, there's a part of me that can't ignore the emptiness that lingers, the loneliness that gnaws at the edges of my solitude. It's a constant presence, one I've grown used to but never fully accepted. I chose this life, but that doesn't mean it doesn't come with its own set of scars.

I pause, leaning on the axe for a moment, and let my thoughts drift back to the past. The missions, the gunfire, the brothers I lost—it's all still there, just beneath the surface, no matter how hard I try to bury it. The PTSD followed me home like a shadow, darkening everything it touched. And then there was Emily. Sweet, patient Evangeline, who tried to love me through the worst of it until she couldn't anymore. She left, and I didn't blame her. I wasn't the man she fell in love with. Hell, I wasn't sure I was even a man anymore. Just a shell, trying to survive.

That's when I came here, to these mountains. Built a life where I didn't have to face the world, where I could pretend I didn't need anything—or anyone. It's worked, for the most part. But lately, the silence feels heavier, the nights longer. And that emptiness, it's harder to ignore.

The crunch of gravel under tires jolts me from my thoughts, pulling me back into the present moment. I straighten my back, the axe still firmly gripped in my hand, as I watch a car maneuver its way up the long, winding road that leads to my secluded cabin. It's not often that I receive visitors—most folks in the area have learned to respect my solitude and keep their distance. But whoever this is, they either don't know my preference for isolation or simply don't care to acknowledge it. A knot of unease forms in my stomach as I wonder what they want and why they've chosen this particular moment to intrude on my carefully constructed solitude.

The car comes to a stop, and for a moment, I consider turning back to my work, letting them figure out on their own that they're not welcome. But curiosity gets the better of me, and I stay where I am, waiting to see who's decided to invade my peace.

When the door swings open and she steps out, and a jolt of irritation courses through me. She's the last person I expected to see in this remote setting—a city girl clad in polished, expensive-looking attire that seems completely out of place among the trees and underbrush. Her black heels sink slightly into the dirt as she stands there, momentarily absorbing the unfamiliar surroundings with a wide-eyed curiosity. Though she's small and almost delicate in appearance, there's a steely determination in her stance that momentarily holds my attention, forcing me to reconsider my initial judgment.

I don't say anything as she approaches, my silence stretching between us like a taut wire. I watch her eyes flit from the cabin to the axe in my hand, and then back to me, each glance conveying a mix of curiosity and confusion. She doesn't look afraid, not at all; rather, she seems to be grappling with the strangeness of the moment, as if she's trying to make sense of her surroundings. And it irritates the hell out of me. What is she doing here, disrupting the solitude I've carved out for myself?

"Hi," she says, her voice steady, though I can see the tension in her jaw. "I'm Natalie Dawson."

I just nod, not offering any response. Her name means nothing to me, and I'm not in the mood for small talk. But there's something in her eyes—something that flickers, almost like uncertainty. And for some reason, that makes me soften—just a little.

"I'm here about the land," she continues, taking another step forward. "I'm working on a project for a photoshoot, and I need your permission to use it."

Of course, she's here for that. They always are, these outsiders with their grand ideas and plans. People who want to take what's mine, to reshape it into something that aligns with their vision of what this place should be, stripping away its essence in the process. I've dealt with her kind before, time and again, and it never ends well. Each encounter leaves a bitter taste, a reminder of the battles fought to preserve what little is left of my sanctuary.

"You've got the wrong guy," I say, my voice flat. "I'm not interested."

I expect her to back off, to realize that she's wasting her time and leave. But she doesn't. She stands her ground, her gaze meeting mine with a steadiness that surprises me. There's no fear there, just determination. And something else, something I can't quite place.

"Look, I understand that you're not interested in outsiders," she says, and there's a hint of frustration in her voice now. "But I really need this, and I'm willing to work with you. I'm not here to cause trouble."

I narrow my eyes, studying her. There's a fire in her that I didn't expect, a stubbornness that's almost... admirable. But that doesn't change the fact that she doesn't belong here, that she's trying to drag the outside world into a place where it has no business being.

"I said no," I repeat, turning back to the log in front of me. I lift the axe, intending to drive the point home, but there's something in the way she's looking at me—something that makes me hesitate.

For the briefest of moments, I feel a pull, a connection that I haven't felt in years. It's unsettling, and I push it aside, focusing on the task at hand. But even as I bring the axe down, splitting the log cleanly in two, I can't shake the feeling that this woman, with her polished shoes and determined smile, is going to be trouble.

"Just leave," I say, not looking at her. "There's nothing for you here."

I expect her to argue, to push back like so many others have before her. But instead, she just stands there, watching me with those eyes that see more than I want them to. Finally, she nods, a small, almost resigned gesture.

"Okay," she says quietly. "But I'll be back."

And with that, she turns and walks back to her car, her heels crunching on the gravel. I watch her go, the irritation slowly fading, replaced by something else—something I can't quite name. As she drives away, I shake my head, trying to rid myself of the strange unease that's settled in my chest.

But it's too late. The peace I found here, in this place I've made my own, has been disrupted. And deep down, I know that things won't be the same after this. Not with her around.

I turn back to my work, but the rhythm is off now, the axe heavier in my hand. As the sound of the car fades into the distance, I'm left with a feeling I haven't had in a long time—one of uncertainty, of something shifting in the carefully constructed life I've built.

And I'm not sure I'm ready for it.

CHAPTER 3

Natalie

I WAKE to the sound of birdsong, a gentle melody that pulls me from sleep. For a moment, I'm disoriented, the unfamiliar quiet settling over me like a thick blanket. No blaring car horns, no city noise—just the soft chirping of birds outside my window. I open my eyes, blinking against the soft golden light filtering through the curtains. The air is cool and crisp, carrying the faintest scent of pine. It's peaceful, almost too peaceful, and I find myself both comforted and unnerved by it.

I push the covers back and slide out of bed, my feet touching the cool wooden floor. The room is simple, cozy, with a quilted bedspread and a small vase of wildflowers on the dresser. It's a far cry from the sleek, modern apartment I left behind, but there's a warmth here that I can't ignore. A warmth that seeps into my bones, making me want to linger, to let my guard down—if only for a moment.

But I can't afford to relax. Not yet. I'm here to work, to prove that I can handle this project and save my career. I glance out the window, taking in the view of Buttercup Bay. The town is bathed in the soft glow of early morning, the rooftops dusted with the gold of autumn leaves. There's a stillness to it, a sense of time slowing down, and for the first time in a long while, I don't feel the usual rush to get moving. I allow myself a few more minutes of quiet before I dress and head out to explore the town.

The air is brisk as I step outside, the autumn chill biting at my cheeks. I pull my coat tighter around me, my heels clicking against the cobblestone streets. It's early, but Buttercup Bay is already coming to life. Golden leaves flutter down from the trees, swirling around my feet as I walk. The porches are decorated with pumpkins and garlands of orange and yellow leaves, and the scent of spiced cider wafts through the air, mingling with the earthy smell of the fallen leaves. It's picturesque, almost too perfect, like something out of a storybook.

But as I walk, I can't shake the feeling of being out of place. My heels echo loudly against the cobblestones, drawing curious glances from the locals. They nod politely as I pass, but I can see the question in their eyes—who is this outsider in their town? I offer a small smile in return, but it feels forced and hollow. I'm used to being a stranger in a crowd, but here, in this close-knit community, it's different. There's a warmth to Buttercup Bay that I haven't experienced in a long time, and I'm not sure how to fit into it.

As I round a corner, the café I went to yesterday comes into view. The windows are fogged with warmth, and the soft murmur of conversation drifts out into the street. I'm drawn to it, the promise of coffee and comfort too tempting to resist. Pushing open the door, I'm greeted by the rich aroma of freshly brewed coffee and baked goods. The warmth envelops me, soothing the tension I didn't realize I was carrying.

Maggie stands behind the counter, her silver hair elegantly pulled back into a neat bun, framing her kind face. Her eyes crinkle in a welcoming smile that radiates warmth and familiarity. "Morning, dear," she says, her voice a soft lilt that dances through the air and instantly puts me at ease. The gentle cadence of her words feels like a hug on a chilly day. "Coffee?"

"Please," I reply, returning her smile as I slide onto a stool at the counter.

She pours me a cup, the steam rising in delicate tendrils. "How are you finding Buttercup Bay so far?"

I wrap my hands around the warm mug, letting the heat seep into my skin. "It's... different," I admit. "Quiet, peaceful. Not what I'm used to."

Maggie nods, her eyes twinkling with understanding. "It takes some getting used to, that's for sure. But there's something special about this place. It has a way of growing on you."

I take a slow sip of my coffee, savoring the rich, smooth flavor that coats my tongue. There's a comforting rhythm to this place, a slower pace that feels foreign yet enticing. Back in the city, life revolves around speed, competition, and the relentless drive for survival. But here, it's different. People take their time; they linger over conversations, sharing stories and laughter as if the world outside is a distant concern. It's unsettling, in a way, because it forces me to question what I've been missing all this time—what it truly means to connect with others beyond the rush of everyday life.

As I take another sip, the door swings open, and a man walks in, his boots thudding heavily on the wooden floor. He's tall, broad-shouldered, with a rugged, weathered face and a playful glint in his eye. "Morning, Maggie," he greets her, his voice deep and warm.

"Morning, Sam," Maggie replies, her smile widening. She gestures to me. "This is Natalie Dawson. She's new in town."

Sam's gaze shifts to me, and I can see the curiosity there, but also something else—an easy warmth that makes me relax a little. "Nice to meet you, Natalie," he says, extending a hand.

I shake it, his grip firm but not overwhelming. "Nice to meet you, too."

He settles onto a stool beside me, his eyes twinkling with amusement. "So, you're the one trying to get Jack Wilder to play nice, huh?"

I blink, surprised by his directness. "I guess you could say that."

Sam chuckles, a rich, hearty sound. "Good luck with that. Jack's a tough nut to crack. Been living up in those mountains so long, I'm not sure he knows how to be social anymore."

Maggie chuckles along with him, but there's a gentleness in her eyes when she looks back at me. "Jack's been through a lot. He's a good man, but he values his privacy. Don't take it personally if he's a bit gruff."

There's a softness in Maggie's voice, a hint of something that makes me curious. "What happened to him?" I ask, my voice cautious, not wanting to pry too much.

Maggie's smile fades a little, her gaze turning inward. "He was in the military. Saw things no one should have to see. Came back different, like a lot of them do. His fiancée, Evangeline, tried to help him, but... well, it was too much. Jack's been on his own ever since."

I feel a pang of sympathy, mingled with an insatiable curiosity about this man who seems so determined to keep the world at arm's length, as if protecting himself from any further pain. "That must have been incredibly hard for him," I say softly, my mind racing with the implications of his past and the weight he carries.

"It was," Maggie agrees softly. "But Jack's strong. He's found his own way to cope, even if it means shutting the rest of us out."

Sam takes a sip of his coffee, his expression thoughtful. "He's not as tough as he likes to pretend, though. Deep down, I think he's just waiting for the right person to knock some sense into him."

I smile at that, though I'm not sure I'm the person who can do it. Jack Wilder sounds like a challenge—a big one. But there's something about the way Maggie and Sam talk about him that makes me want to try. Not just for the project, but because I can sense there's more to him than the gruff exterior.

As I finish my coffee, the café's warmth seeps into me, relaxing the tension in my shoulders. The conversation with Maggie and Sam has given me more than just information—it's given me a glimpse into the heart of this town. Buttercup Bay is more than just a pretty backdrop; it's a community, a place where people care about each other, where they take the time to connect. It's a stark contrast to the life I've known, a life built on ambition and competition, where success is measured by how fast you can climb the ladder.

But here, in this small town adorned with golden leaves that dance in the crisp autumn breeze and the warm embrace of spiced cider wafting through the air, I'm beginning to see that there's another way to live. A way that's slower and more intentional, where success isn't measured by the number of achievements or accolades amassed, but by the depth of connections forged with those around you. And for the first time in a long time, I find myself wondering if maybe, just maybe, I've been searching for the wrong thing all along, chasing after fleeting goals instead of nurturing the relationships that could truly enrich my life.

As I step back out into the crisp autumn air, my heels clicking against the cobblestones once more, I feel a little lighter, a little more open to the possibilities that Buttercup Bay might hold. The challenge with Jack is daunting, but I'm not ready to give up. There's something here worth exploring, something that goes beyond just saving my career.

And as I walk back toward the inn, the golden leaves swirling around me like a gentle reminder of the season's change, I find myself smiling. Buttercup Bay is starting to grow on me, and the thought isn't as unsettling as it was before. It's... comforting, in a way I didn't expect. Maybe there's more for me here than I realized.

CHAPTER 4

Jack

THE STEADY RHYTHM of the axe hitting the wood is a familiar comfort. The solid thunk as the blade sinks into the log, the satisfying crack as it splits in two. Out here, in the quiet of the mountains, it's easy to lose myself in the work. The air is cool, carrying the scent of pine and earth, and the only sounds are the rustle of leaves and the distant call of a bird. This is my sanctuary—a place where the world doesn't intrude, where I can keep everything at a distance.

But today, the stillness is shattered by the low hum of an engine, cutting through the quiet. I pause, wiping the sweat from my brow with the back of my hand, and look up just in time to see the familiar car making its way up the road. Her car.

Natalie Dawson. The moment I spot the vehicle, an unsettling mix of irritation and curiosity tightens in my chest like a vice. What is she doing here again, intruding on my solitary retreat? I thought I had made it abundantly clear that I wasn't interested in her company or the complications that come with it. Yet, here she is, as persistent and determined as ever, refusing to take the hint. It's almost as if she thrives on my discomfort, somehow sensing my annoyance from afar and choosing to parade right into it.

I plant the axe in the stump and wait, my arms crossed over my chest, as the car rolls to a stop. The engine cuts off, and for a moment, there's nothing but silence. Then the door opens, and Natalie steps out, her heels sinking slightly into the dirt, just like the last time. But there's something different today. Maybe it's the determined set of her shoulders, or the way her gaze sweeps across my property with a look of resolve. Whatever it is, it's clear she's not going to back down easily.

She approaches with purpose, her stride confident despite the uneven ground. I can't help but admire her tenacity, even if it does irritate the hell out of me. Most people would have taken my refusal and left it at that, but not her. There's a stubbornness in her that I recognize, and maybe that's part of what bothers me. It's like looking in a mirror.

"Natalie," I say, my tone flat as I try to keep my expression neutral. "You're back."

She stops a few feet away, her eyes meeting mine with that same determined spark. "I told you I would be."

I grunt, caught off guard and unsure how to respond. She's here, standing on my land again, defying my earlier rejection, and I can't deny the flicker of something that stirs deep within me— something I haven't felt in a long time. It's unsettling, a reminder of emotions I'd rather keep buried. I push it aside forcefully, clinging to my irritation instead, as if it can shield me from whatever this unexpected reaction might mean.

"I thought I made it clear," I say, keeping my voice low and even. "I'm not interested in your project."

Natalie doesn't flinch at my words. Instead, she takes a deliberate step closer, her chin lifting slightly in a gesture that's more defiant than confrontational, as if she's challenging me to reconsider my stance without raising her voice. "I understand that," she replies, her tone steady and unwavering. "But I'm not here to argue. I'm here to help." The conviction in her voice is palpable, and it sends a ripple of uncertainty through me, making it harder to maintain my resolve.

"Help?" I echo, narrowing my eyes. "With what, exactly?"

She glances at the axe still lodged in the stump, then back at me. "With whatever you're doing. Chopping wood, fixing things—I'm willing to work with you if you'll just give me a chance."

I can't help the slight raise of my eyebrow at the unexpected image that forms in my mind. The thought of this polished city girl, with her immaculate attire and refined demeanor, swinging an axe like a seasoned lumberjack is almost laughable, yet the sincerity in her voice makes me pause. There's a depth to her conviction that I can't easily dismiss. She's serious. She's truly willing to roll up her sleeves, leave her comfort zone behind, and get her hands dirty in a way I never would have anticipated.

"Look," she continues, taking my silence as an invitation to keep talking. "I know I'm not exactly... cut out for this kind of work, but I'm not afraid to try. Let me help, and maybe you'll see that I'm not just some outsider trying to impose on your life."

I stare at her, weighing my options. She's stubborn, I'll give her that. And there's a part of me—a very small part—that's curious. Curious about why she's so determined, about what's driving her. But more than that, there's something in the way she's looking at me that softens the edges of my irritation. Maybe it's the genuine effort she's putting in, or the fact that she's not turning tail and running like most people would.

"All right," I say finally, surprising even myself. "But don't say I didn't warn you."

A flicker of relief washes over her face, and she nods in agreement, a small smile tugging at the corners of her lips as if a weight has been lifted. "I won't," she assures me, her voice steady and sincere, a hint of determination shining through her expression.

I pull the axe from the stump, the sound of the blade scraping against the wood echoing in the stillness of the moment, and hold it out to her. For just a fleeting moment, she hesitates, uncertainty flickering in her eyes, but then she reaches out and takes it, her fingers brushing against mine as she firmly grips the handle. The axe is heavy, far too heavy for someone who's clearly never attempted this before, but she doesn't voice any complaints. Instead, with an unexpected spark of determination igniting her expression, she lifts it, her arms straining slightly as she adjusts her stance, trying to position herself the way she's observed me do it. The muscles in her arms quiver with the effort, but there's a fire in her gaze that suggests she's ready to face the challenge head-on.

"Like this?" she asks, her voice laced with uncertainty.

I nod, stepping closer to adjust her stance. "Not quite. Here, let me show you."

I place my hands over hers, gently guiding her movements as she struggles to swing the axe. Her hands are soft and delicate, and the smoothness of her skin contrasts starkly against the rough, splintered wood of the handle. A brief, strange thrill courses through me at the contact, a sensation I quickly push aside, aware that now is not the time for distractions. I focus intently on the task at hand, demonstrating how to bring the axe down with just the right amount of force, ensuring she understands the rhythm and precision required for each swing.

She tries a few more times, each attempt a little better than the last, but it's clear she's struggling. Her face flushes from the effort, and I can see the beginnings of blisters forming on her hands. Part of me wants to tell her to stop, to take the axe from her and send her on her way, but another part—the part that's starting to enjoy her company—keeps quiet.

Finally, after what feels like an eternity of focused effort and determination, she manages to split a log in half. It's a clumsy, uneven cut, jagged along the edges, but it's a cut nonetheless, a tangible testament to her perseverance. She steps back, her chest heaving as she catches her breath, and looks up at me with a triumphant grin that lights up her face, a mixture of pride and disbelief dancing in her eyes.

"See?" she says, her voice breathless. "I can learn."

I can't help the reluctant smile that tugs at my lips. There's something infectious about her determination, something that makes me forget, just for a moment, why I've kept people at arm's length for so long.

"You did all right," I admit, nodding toward the log she split. "But don't push yourself. You'll end up with blisters the size of quarters if you keep going like that."

She glances down at her hands, wincing slightly. "Too late."

Without thinking, I reach out and take her hands in mine, gently turning them over to inspect the damage. Her skin is red and raw in places, evidence of her determination, and I can see the blisters starting to form, tiny, angry bubbles threatening to burst. "You're going to need some salve for that," I mutter, more to myself than to her, feeling a rush of concern wash over me. "Come on, I've got some in the cabin." I squeeze her hands lightly as if to reassure both of us that she'll be okay.

She follows me inside without a word, and as I lead her to the small kitchen where I keep my first aid supplies, I realize how strange this feels—having someone else in my space, someone who isn't just passing through. It's unsettling, but it's also... nice.

I find the salve and gesture for her to sit at the table. She does, holding out her hands as I carefully apply the ointment. The silence between us is comfortable now, the awkwardness from earlier fading as we settle into this unexpected rhythm.

"Thank you," she says quietly, watching me with those wide, curious eyes. "For letting me stay."

I shrug, focusing on my task. "Figured it was easier than arguing with you."

She chuckles softly, the sound light and musical, a gentle melody that dances in the air between us. I feel something warm unfurl in my chest, a sensation that spreads like sunlight breaking through clouds on a dreary day. It's been a long time since I've allowed myself the luxury of enjoying someone's company like this, to share a moment without the weight of the world pressing down. The realization is both comforting and terrifying, a delicate balance that leaves me breathless, teetering on the edge of vulnerability.

As I finish with her hands, I can't help but notice the way she's looking at me—not with fear or pity, but with genuine interest. It stirs something in me, something I've kept buried for so long that I almost forgot it was there. It's a feeling of connection, of wanting to share more of myself with someone, even though I know it's dangerous.

"You're different from most people who come here," I say finally, meeting her gaze. "Most of them don't bother to try."

She tilts her head, a small smile playing on her lips. "Maybe I'm just stubborn."

"Maybe," I agree, though I know there's more to it than that. There's a strength in her, a resilience that I can't help but admire. And as much as it scares me, I'm drawn to it, to her, in a way that I haven't been drawn to anyone in a long time.

But with that attraction comes fear. Fear of what it means to let someone in, to open myself up to the possibility of connection—and the pain that could come with it. I've spent years building walls around myself, walls that have kept me safe, if not happy. And now, with Natalie standing here in my cabin, those walls are starting to crack.

I look away, focusing on putting the salve back in its place, trying to regain some control over the situation. "You should probably head back," I say, my voice gruff again. "Give your hands a chance to heal."

She nods, though there's a hint of disappointment in her eyes. "I will. But I'll be back tomorrow."

I don't argue. Part of me wants to, but another part —the part that's slowly warming to her presence— just nods in acceptance. "Tomorrow, then."

As she leaves, I watch her go, that same strange mix of emotions churning in my chest. She's persistent, I'll give her that. And for the first time in a long time, I'm not entirely sure I want her to leave. Not yet.

The silence of the cabin settles around me like a thick blanket as the sound of her car fades into the distance, but it's not the same as before. It's... different. There's a new energy in the air, a palpable shift that both excites and terrifies me. It feels as though the walls are holding their breath, waiting for something to happen, for a change to take root in this quiet space. The stillness now carries a weight, a promise of possibilities that I hadn't considered before, mingling with the unease that stirs deep within me.

And as I pick up the axe again, the weight of it familiar in my hands, I can't shake the feeling that things are changing. That maybe, just maybe, I'm ready to let those walls come down.

CHAPTER 5

Natalie

BUTTERCUP BAY IS a whirlwind of activity as the town enthusiastically gears up for the highly anticipated annual Halloween Bash. The energy is infectious, buzzing through the crisp autumn air like a lively melody, and I can't help but be drawn into it, swept away by the vibrant atmosphere. The town square is alive with an explosion of color—golden leaves drift lazily from the branches of towering oaks, children's laughter fills the air as they eagerly carve pumpkins with gleeful determination, and vendors busily set up their stalls, overflowing with an array of homemade crafts, intricate decorations, and mouthwatering baked goods. The scent of warm cinnamon and freshly baked bread wafts through the air, mingling delightfully with the sharp, tangy aroma of cider, creating a sensory tapestry that wraps around me. It's like something out of a storybook, a picturesque scene crafted by an artist's hand, and for a moment, I feel as though I've stepped into a different world altogether, where magic and joy intertwine seamlessly in the spirit of the season.

Maggie catches my eye from across the square, waving me over with a warm smile. "Natalie, dear! Come on, I've got just the thing for you."

I weave through the crowd, the sound of my heels clicking against the cobblestones drowned out by the cheerful noise around me. When I reach Maggie, she hands me a basket filled with small pumpkins and a spool of orange ribbon.

"We're decorating the square," she explains, her eyes twinkling with mischief. "And I need all the help I can get. Besides, it'll give you a chance to get to know some of the locals—and maybe convince that stubborn Jack to pitch in."

I laugh, shaking my head. "You're relentless, you know that?"

Maggie just grins. "You'll thank me later."

As I move to a quieter corner of the square to start arranging the pumpkins, I can't help but think about Jack. He's been on my mind more than I'd like to admit, and the way he let me stay yesterday—teaching me how to chop wood, patching up my blisters—has only deepened my curiosity about him. There's a part of me that wants to know more, to break through the walls he's built around himself, even though I know it's risky.

I'm lost in thought, carefully tying a vibrant ribbon around a plump pumpkin, when an unsettling sense of presence pricks at my awareness. I turn, startled, and find Jack standing there, a few feet away. His hands are shoved deep into his pockets, and his expression is a mask, making it difficult for me to decipher what he's feeling. The autumn breeze tousles his hair slightly, adding an air of casualness to the moment that contrasts with the tension simmering just beneath the surface.

"You need help?" he asks, his voice gruff but not unkind.

I smile, a warmth spreading through me at the sight of him. "I wouldn't say no."

He steps closer, taking the basket from me and setting it down. As he kneels beside me, I can't help but notice the way his hands move with such ease and precision, even with something as simple as arranging pumpkins. There's a quiet strength in him, a connection to the world around him that I find both comforting and intimidating.

"I didn't expect you to come," I admit as we work side by side, our hands occasionally brushing against each other.

He shrugs, his gaze focused on the task at hand. "Figured I owed you for yesterday."

I glance at him, my curiosity piqued as I attempt to decipher the emotions hidden behind his carefully composed expression. He remains as guarded as ever, a fortress of stoicism that has become familiar to me. Yet, there's a softness in his voice that wasn't there before, a subtle warmth that wraps around his words like a gentle embrace. It gives me a flicker of hope, a fragile yet persistent thought that maybe, just maybe, he's beginning to let me in, allowing the walls he has built to crumble, even if just a little.

As we finish arranging the pumpkins, Maggie reappears, her eyes sparkling with approval. "Looks like you two make a good team," she says, her tone light but knowing.

Jack grunts, but there's a hint of a smile on his lips as he stands. "Don't get used to it."

Maggie just laughs, patting him on the arm. "Oh, Jack, you're a softie at heart, even if you won't admit it."

He mutters something under his breath, but I can see the faint flush of color on his cheeks. It's endearing, and I find myself smiling as he walks away, heading toward another group of townspeople who need help setting up hay bales.

Maggie turns to me, her smile turning a little more serious. "He's a good man, Natalie. Just needs someone to remind him of that every once in a while."

"I can see that," I reply, my thoughts drifting back to the way he carefully tended to my hands, the unexpected gentleness in his touch.

Maggie gives me a knowing look before she's pulled away by another volunteer. I watch her go, feeling a mix of emotions—hope, confusion, and something deeper that I'm not quite ready to name.

AS THE DAY WEARS ON, the square becomes even more vibrant. The children's laughter rings out as they chase each other around the decorated stalls, their faces smeared with pumpkin guts and wide smiles. The scent of freshly baked pies drifts through the air, making my stomach growl, and I catch sight of Jack again, this time helping a group of men string up lights around the square.

I decide to join him, picking up a string of twinkling lights that seem to shimmer even in the daylight. With a determined step, I walk over, feeling a flutter of anticipation in my stomach. He glances at me, one eyebrow raised in question, a hint of surprise flickering across his face, but he doesn't say anything as I start helping him hang the lights. It's a simple task, just wrapping the strands around the wooden beams and securing them with cheerful clips, but the proximity to him, the quiet camaraderie that settles comfortably between us, makes it feel like so much more. Each time our hands brush against one another as we work, a spark of unspoken connection ignites, deepening the moment into something sweetly significant.

"Have you always lived in Buttercup Bay?" I ask after a while, breaking the comfortable silence.

He hesitates for a moment before nodding. "Grew up here. Left for a while, but came back after... everything."

His voice trails off, and I don't press him. Instead, I focus on the lights, careful not to tangle them as we work our way around the square. But I can't stop thinking about what he said, about the pain that lingers in his words.

"Do you ever think about leaving again?" I ask, keeping my tone light.

Jack pauses, looking out over the square, his expression thoughtful. "Sometimes," he admits quietly. "But this is home. It's where I belong."

There's a conviction in his voice that tugs at something deep inside me. I've spent so much of my life chasing success, moving from place to place, never really feeling like I belong anywhere. And here's Jack, so deeply rooted in this small town, in this life he's built for himself. It's both admirable and terrifying, because it makes me wonder if I've been searching for the wrong things all along.

"What about you?" Jack asks, turning the question back on me. "You ever think about settling down somewhere?"

I hesitate, unsure how to answer. "I'm not sure," I finally say. "I've always been focused on my career, on proving myself. But lately..."

He waits, his gaze steady, and I feel a sudden urge to be honest with him, to share the doubts that have been creeping up on me since I arrived in Buttercup Bay.

"Lately, I've been wondering if there's more to life than just work," I admit, my voice barely above a whisper. "If maybe I've been so focused on success that I've missed out on something important."

Jack doesn't say anything, but the understanding in his eyes speaks volumes. We finish hanging the lights in silence, but it's a comfortable silence, one that feels like an unspoken agreement—a shared understanding that we're both searching for something, even if we don't know what it is yet.

As the sun begins to set, casting a warm orange glow over the square, I find myself irresistibly drawn back to the pumpkin carving station. The vibrant laughter of the children has long since faded, replaced now by the soft murmur of adults enjoying the evening's gentle ambiance. Conversations flow easily, punctuated by the occasional burst of laughter as friends reconnect and share stories. Jack follows me, his presence a steady comfort that anchors me amidst the shifting atmosphere, and I can feel the warmth of his support even without a word exchanged between us.

"Think you can show me how to carve one of these properly?" I ask, gesturing to the pile of pumpkins.

He smiles, the first real smile I've seen from him, and nods. "Let's see what you've got."

We sit side by side, the cool air nipping at our cheeks as we pick out our pumpkins. Jack hands me a carving knife, his fingers brushing against mine, and I can't help the flutter in my chest at the brief contact.

"Start by cutting off the top," he instructs, demonstrating with his own pumpkin. I follow his lead, my movements tentative at first, but Jack's calm presence gives me the confidence to continue.

As we work, our conversation flows more easily, the barriers between us slowly breaking down. Jack tells me about the festivals he attended as a kid and the way the whole town would come together to celebrate. There's a fondness in his voice, a connection to this place that runs deep.

"I used to think these festivals were silly," he admits, his hands steady as he carves a jagged grin into his pumpkin. "But now, I see the value in them. It's about more than just the celebration—it's about community, about coming together."

I nod, understanding what he means. There's a warmth in Buttercup Bay that I haven't felt anywhere else, a sense of belonging that's hard to ignore. And as I carve my pumpkin, guided by Jack's gentle instructions, I start to realize that my attraction to him isn't just physical. It's deeper than that, rooted in his strength, his integrity, and the vulnerability he tries so hard to hide.

But with that realization comes a wave of uncertainty. Falling for Jack would mean more than just a change in my relationship status—it would mean a complete upheaval of the life I've built in the city. A life I've worked so hard to create, a life that defines who I am.

As we finish our pumpkins, Jack looks over at mine, a lopsided grin on his face. "Not bad for a city girl."

I laugh, the sound genuine and light, and for a moment, all my doubts and fears fade away. "I had a good teacher."

We set our pumpkins alongside the others, the flickering candles inside casting eerie shadows on the ground. The square is quiet now, the festival preparations winding down as the town prepares for the big event tomorrow. But the connection I feel with Jack is stronger than ever, and it scares me—because I know that if I let myself fall for him, I'll have to make a choice.

And I'm not sure I'm ready to make that leap.

As the evening air grows colder, a crisp chill settling around us, Jack walks me back to the inn. The dim glow of the streetlights casts a warm halo around us, making the world feel smaller and more intimate. We don't talk much, but the silence between us is comfortable, wrapped in the gentle rhythm of our footsteps. It is filled with the unspoken understanding that something is shifting, something important—a delicate tension that seems to hum in the air, urging us to acknowledge the bond that is quietly deepening with each passing moment.

When we reach the inn, Jack pauses, his gaze lingering on me for a moment longer than usual. "See you tomorrow?"

I nod, my heart pounding in my chest. "Tomorrow."

He gives me a small, almost shy smile before turning and walking away, his figure disappearing into the darkness. I watch him go, my mind racing with all the possibilities, all the risks and rewards that come with falling for someone like Jack.

And as I step inside the inn, the warmth of the fire greeting me, I can't help but wonder what tomorrow will bring—and whether I'm ready to face it.

CHAPTER 6

Jack

THE NEXT DAY, Natalie arrives at my place, her presence radiating an infectious energy that instantly brightens the atmosphere. Without much thought, I suggest we go for a hike, the idea popping into my mind as a spontaneous way to spend time together. To my surprise, she enthusiastically agrees, her eyes lighting up with excitement, even though I notice she isn't quite dressed for the outdoors. Her outfit, more suited for a casual day in the city than a trek through nature, adds a touch of charm to the moment, making me wonder what adventures await us on the trail.

The trail ahead is narrow, winding through the dense forest like a secret path known only to those who belong here. I've walked it countless times, but today, the journey feels different. I can hear Natalie's footsteps behind me, light and careful as she navigates the uneven ground. The scent of damp earth fills the air, mingling with the crisp, clean smell of pine. It's a familiar comfort, grounding me in this wild place that feels like an extension of myself.

The forest is alive with the rustle of leaves and the occasional call of a bird. The sound of our footsteps is muted by the soft, mossy ground, and the only other noise is the steady rhythm of our breathing. Out here, in the wilderness, I feel at home. The wildness of the land mirrors the parts of me I've kept hidden, the untamed edges that I've tried so hard to control.

I glance back at Natalie, watching as she steps carefully over a gnarled root. Her cheeks are flushed from the exertion, but there's a determined set to her jaw that I can't help but admire. She's out of her element, yet she's not backing down. There's a resilience in her that stirs something deep inside me, something I've tried to bury for a long time.

"Almost there," I say, my voice low but steady. She

nods, offering a small smile, and I turn back to the trail, leading her deeper into the mountains.

The path narrows as we climb, the forest closing in around us. The trees are tall and ancient, their branches reaching out like protective arms. I've always felt safe here, away from the noise and chaos of the world. But today, with Natalie by my side, I feel a different kind of safety—a sense of belonging that I haven't felt in years.

We reach a small clearing, where a stream cuts through the forest, its water clear and cold as it rushes over smooth stones. I stop by the edge, setting down the pack I brought with us, and turn to Natalie. She's looking around, taking in the beauty of the place, and I can see the awe in her eyes.

"It's beautiful," she whispers, her voice barely above the sound of the stream.

I nod, feeling a rare warmth in my chest. "It's my favorite spot."

She kneels by the water, her delicate fingers gliding through the cool, rippling surface as if trying to capture the essence of the moment. I watch her for a moment, captivated, feeling a tug in my chest that's both comforting and terrifying. She doesn't belong here, not in this wild, untamed place that seems to pulse with the heartbeat of the earth, yet there's an undeniable part of me that wants her to stay. A part of me that's beginning to crave her presence, her laughter mingling with the sound of the stream, despite the risks that loom like shadows in my mind.

I sit down beside her, pulling out a small tin box from the pack. "Here," I say, opening it to reveal an assortment of dried herbs. "I wanted to show you something."

She leans closer, her curiosity piqued. "What's this?"

"Wild herbs," I explain, picking up a small bundle of dried leaves. "This one's yarrow. Good for wounds—stops the bleeding and helps with healing."

She listens intently as I go through the different herbs, explaining their uses and how to identify them. There's a satisfaction in teaching her, in sharing this knowledge that's been a part of my life for so long. But there's also a vulnerability in it, a sense of letting her in a little deeper, of showing her a piece of myself that I usually keep hidden.

"Why did you learn all this?" she asks, her voice soft, almost hesitant.

I pause, considering how much to share. But the openness in her eyes, the genuine interest, makes it easier to speak. "After I came back from the military, I needed something to ground me. Something that connected me to the world in a way that didn't involve people. The mountains gave me that. The herbs, the land—they became my way of healing."

She nods, her gaze never leaving mine. "And it worked?"

"Mostly," I admit, the word heavy with the weight of everything I haven't said. "But some scars don't heal."

We lapse into silence, the only sound the gentle rush of the stream. It's a comfortable quiet, one that feels like an unspoken understanding between us. I cast my fishing line into the water, watching the way it ripples through the current. Natalie follows suit, her movements a little awkward but determined. There's something about her persistence, her willingness to try, that makes me want to open up in a way I haven't before.

"It wasn't just the military," I say after a while, my voice barely audible over the sound of the water. "There was someone else. Evangeline. We were engaged before I left. When I came back, I wasn't the same person. She tried to help, but it was too much. She left."

Natalie doesn't say anything, but I can feel her eyes on me, full of quiet empathy. It's not pity—there's a difference, and I can tell. She's listening, really listening, and it makes it easier to keep going.

"After that, I decided it was better to be alone. Safer, you know? No one to hurt, no one to disappoint." I swallow hard, the words tasting bitter on my tongue. "But it gets lonely."

She reaches out, her hand brushing against mine in a gesture that feels both gentle and grounding, as if she's anchoring me to the present moment. "I can't imagine what you've been through," she says softly, her voice filled with sincerity. "But I do know what it's like to be afraid of letting people in, to keep walls built high to protect yourself from the pain of loss or betrayal."

I glance at her, surprised by the raw honesty in her voice. She's always seemed so confident, so put-together, but there's a vulnerability in her now that I didn't expect.

"I've spent so much time trying to prove myself," she continues, her gaze focused on the water. "To show the world that I can succeed, that I'm strong and independent. But sometimes... sometimes I wonder if I'm just running from the fear of being alone. Of not knowing where I truly belong."

Her words resonate with me, striking a chord deep inside. I've always believed that solitude was safer, that it was better to live alone than to risk the pain of loss. But hearing her speak, seeing the reflection of my own fears in her eyes, makes me question whether I've been running from life rather than living it.

"Natalie," I say, my voice rough with emotion, "you do belong. Maybe it's not where you thought, but you're not alone."

She looks at me then, really looks at me, and I can see the tears glistening in her eyes. "Thank you," she whispers, her voice trembling with the weight of everything she's feeling.

We sit in silence for a while longer, the bond between us growing stronger with every shared word, every quiet moment. The wilderness around us feels like a living, breathing entity, a silent witness to the connection that's forming between us. It's a connection I didn't expect, one that scares me because it's real, and it's here, and I don't know if I'm ready for it.

But as the sun begins to dip lower in the sky, casting a warm, golden light that dances through the leaves and blankets the forest floor in a soft glow, I realize that maybe, just maybe, I'm tired of running. The weight of my past has become a burden I can no longer carry alone. Perhaps it's time to stop hiding behind the walls I've meticulously constructed, to let someone in, even if it means risking the pain that inevitably accompanies such vulnerability. The thought sends a shiver down my spine, a mixture of fear and hope swirling within me, urging me to take that leap into the unknown.

Natalie glances at me, her expression soft and open. "I'm glad you brought me here, Jack."

"Me too," I admit, the words surprising me with their sincerity.

As we gather our things and start the hike back down the mountain, the air is filled with the sounds of the forest—birds singing, leaves rustling, the distant call of a deer. But there's a new sound, too, one that I haven't heard in a long time: the sound of hope.

And for the first time in years, I feel like I'm not running anymore. I'm just living.

CHAPTER 7

Natalie

THE SKY outside Jack's cabin darkens ominously, thick clouds rolling in like a foreboding warning. I glance out the window, watching intently as the first snowflakes drift lazily to the ground, each one a tiny, intricate masterpiece. It's almost beautiful—the way the snow flutters down in soft, delicate patterns, swirling gently as it descends. But beneath that beauty, there's a heaviness in the air, an unsettling sense of something more ominous lurking just beyond the horizon, ready to descend upon the tranquil landscape.

"I should get going before it gets worse," I say, turning away from the window. My voice is steady, but there's a hint of unease that I can't quite shake.

Jack looks up from where he's been stacking firewood by the hearth, his expression unreadable. "Might be too late for that," he replies, his voice low and calm, but I can hear the concern underlying his words.

I glance back outside, and my heart skips a beat. The snow has already begun to fall more heavily, thickening into a dense curtain of white that blurs the world beyond the cabin, transforming the familiar landscape into an almost ethereal realm. The wind picks up, rattling the windows with an unsettling ferocity, and I realize with a sinking feeling that leaving isn't an option anymore. The isolation wraps around me like a thick blanket, and a sense of foreboding settles in my chest, reminding me that the world outside is no longer within my reach.

"What started as a light flurry is now a full-blown storm, and it's only getting worse," Jack says, echoing my thoughts.

I nod, trying to push down the sudden surge of anxiety. "Looks like I'm staying."

Jack doesn't respond, but there's a tension in the air now, a quiet anticipation that makes my pulse quicken. The warmth of the fire contrasts sharply with the cold reality outside, creating a cocoon of heat that should be comforting, but all I can focus on is the tension between us—neither of us sure how to navigate the emotions that have been building.

I move closer to the fire, holding my hands out to the flames, trying to soak in as much warmth as I can. The storm rages on outside, the wind howling through the trees, making the cabin feel even smaller, more intimate. The flickering light casts shadows on the walls, the dancing flames reflecting the turmoil inside me.

Jack comes to stand beside me, his presence solid and reassuring, yet it only intensifies the storm of emotions swirling in my chest. I can feel the heat radiating from his body, the subtle brush of his arm against mine, and it takes everything in me to stay still, to not lean into him, to not let the walls I've built around my heart crumble.

The silence stretches on, thick with unspoken words, until it becomes unbearable. I can't hold back any longer. The fear, the longing, the confusion—it all comes rushing to the surface, and before I can stop myself, the words spill out.

"Jack, I—" My voice catches, trembling with the weight of what I'm about to say. "I don't know what I'm doing anymore. I came here to prove something to myself, to show that I could succeed, that I didn't need anyone. But now... now I'm not so sure."

I turn to face him, searching his eyes for some sign of understanding, some glimmer of empathy that might indicate he shares in my turmoil. His expression is guarded, a fortress built from years of his own struggles, yet there's a flicker of something deeper lurking beneath the surface—something that gives me the courage to keep going, a hint of connection that makes me believe he might truly hear me.

"I'm scared, Jack," I confess, my voice barely above a whisper. "I'm scared of falling for someone who might not want the same things, scared of giving up everything I know for a life that's still uncertain. I'm scared of... of getting hurt."

Jack's eyes darken, and I can see the conflict in his gaze, the way his emotions war with his instincts. He's listening, but he's also struggling, and that only makes my heart ache more.

"I don't know what to do," I continue, my voice breaking. "I don't want to lose myself, but I don't want to lose you either."

The words hang in the air between us, heavy and charged with emotion. For a moment, I think he's going to turn away, that he's going to retreat behind the walls he's built around himself. But then he moves, reaching out to gently cup my face in his hand. The warmth of his touch sends a shiver through me, a stark contrast to the cold fear that has taken root in my chest.

"Natalie," he says, his voice rough with emotion. "I've spent so long being afraid of letting someone in, of losing someone I care about. But with you... it's different. I don't want to push you away. I don't want to lose you either."

His words are like a lifeline, pulling me back from the edge of my fear. I can see the vulnerability in his eyes, the way he's battling his own demons, and it breaks something open inside me. The tension between us reaches a breaking point, and suddenly, I can't hold back anymore.

I close the distance between us, my hands fisting in the soft fabric of his shirt as I pull him closer, feeling the warmth radiating from his body. For a heartbeat, we're frozen in time, suspended in the intensity of the moment, our breaths mingling in the charged air around us. Then, without hesitation, our lips crash together in a kiss that's as desperate as it is passionate, overflowing with longing. It's a kiss that's been building for days, maybe even weeks, a slow burn fueled by all the emotions we've been holding back. In that instant, everything else fades away, and all that remains is the rush of heat and the undeniable need that binds us together.

The world outside vanishes, the storm howling in the distance, the biting cold retreating into nothingness, until there is only Jack and me, entwined in each other's arms. His hands glide down to my waist, drawing me even closer as the kiss deepens, our breaths entwining in the narrow space that separates us. The fire crackles behind us, sending flickering shadows dancing across the walls and casting a warm, golden glow over the intimate scene. Yet, all I can truly feel is the blaze that has ignited within me, a heat that surges through my veins like an unstoppable wildfire, consuming everything in its path and leaving only the intoxicating connection that binds us together.

When we finally pull apart, we're both breathless, our foreheads resting together as we try to steady ourselves, savoring the lingering sensation of our closeness. My heart is pounding in my chest, a wild rhythm that mirrors the storm still raging outside, its fury echoing against the walls of the cabin. Yet the fear that had gripped me earlier, a chilling hold that seemed unrelenting, has started to ebb away, replaced by a warmth that's even more powerful, spreading through me like liquid sunshine, illuminating the shadows of doubt and filling me with a sense of safety I never knew I craved.

"Natalie," Jack whispers, his voice rough and low. "This... us... it scares me too. But I don't want to run from it."

I look up at him, my eyes searching his, and in that moment, I see everything I've been afraid to admit—hope, desire, and something deeper, something that feels like the beginning of something real.

"I don't want to run either," I reply, my voice trembling with the weight of the truth I've just admitted. "Not from you."

We stand there, holding onto each other as the storm howls outside, the fire crackling behind us.

The world may be a blur of white and cold, but inside this cabin, inside this moment, everything feels warm and clear. The fear, the uncertainty—it's still there, but it's overshadowed by something stronger. Something that feels like the start of a new beginning.

And as we lean in for another kiss, I know that whatever comes next, we'll face it together.

CHAPTER 8

Jack

THE WORLD outside my cabin has been transformed overnight. The storm that raged through the night has left behind a blanket of pristine white, covering everything in a soft, undisturbed layer of snow. The sun is just starting to rise, casting a golden glow over the snow-covered trees, making them sparkle like they're dusted with diamonds. It's the kind of morning that usually brings me a deep sense of peace—a reminder of why I chose this life, why I sought out the solitude of the mountains.

But today, that peace feels like a distant memory, slipping through my fingers like the delicate snowflakes melting in the rising sun. I sit on the edge of the bed, the chill of the cold morning air wrapping around me like an unwelcome embrace, and all I can think about is last night. The warmth of Natalie's body pressed against mine lingered in my mind, a sweet reminder of her closeness. I can still feel the softness of her lips brushing against my skin, the way she looked at me with such raw vulnerability that it took my breath away. It was a moment of connection, of intimacy, that I haven't allowed myself to truly feel in years, buried beneath the weight of solitude and self-imposed distance.

And now, in the quiet light of morning, it terrifies me.

I've spent so long building walls around myself, keeping people out to protect my heart from the pain of loss. Vulnerability isn't something I've ever been comfortable with, and last night shattered the careful distance I've maintained. I felt something—something real, something deep—and that scares the hell out of me.

I stand abruptly, needing to do something, anything, to keep from thinking about the way her lips felt against mine or the way she looked at me like I was someone worth loving. I pull on my boots and jacket, avoiding the mirror, avoiding the reflection of a man who's suddenly not so sure of the life he's built.

The cabin is quiet as I step out into the snow, the cold biting at my skin, but it's a welcome distraction. The chores need to be done—wood needs to be chopped, the path cleared. Busywork, that's all it is, but it keeps my hands moving, keeps my mind from wandering back to the woman still sleeping inside.

The snow crunches underfoot as I head to the woodpile, grabbing the axe with a bit more force than necessary. I set to work, the rhythmic thud of the axe splitting wood echoing through the stillness. It's a familiar motion, one that usually brings me a sense of control, of order. But today, it feels hollow.

I can't stop thinking about Natalie, about the way she trusted me with her fears, the way she opened up to me in a way I never expected. She's scared of losing herself, of giving up everything she knows for something uncertain. I get that—I feel it too. But the difference is I've spent years running from that uncertainty, convincing myself that solitude was safer.

But now, with Natalie, I'm not so sure.

The wind picks up, swirling the snow around me, but I barely notice. My thoughts are a storm of their own, conflicting emotions battling for dominance. I want to pull her close, to protect her, to let her in. But the fear is there, too, gnawing at the edges of my resolve. If I let her in, I'm risking everything—the peace, the solitude, the control I've fought so hard to maintain.

But more than that, I'm risking my heart. And that's something I'm not sure I can do again.

I'm lost in thought when I hear the crunch of footsteps behind me, the sound cutting through the swirling silence of the falling snow. I turn to see Sam making his way through the thick blanket of white, his breath coming out in puffs of steam that hang in the chilly air like fleeting ghosts. He's a welcome distraction, a familiar presence in this cold landscape, but I can't shake the feeling of unease. I know that once he's close enough, he'll bring with him a barrage of questions that probe at the very heart of my turmoil. Am I truly ready to face those inquiries, to unravel the knot of emotions that I've been so desperately trying to keep at bay?

"Morning," he calls out, his voice carrying easily in the stillness.

"Morning," I reply, setting the axe down as he approaches.

Sam looks around, taking in the freshly split wood and the snow-covered landscape. "Beautiful morning," he says, though there's an edge to his voice that tells me he's here for more than just small talk.

"Yeah," I mutter, not meeting his gaze. I can feel his eyes on me, sharp and assessing, and I know he's picking up on the tension I'm trying to hide.

"You gonna tell me what's got you out here chopping wood like you're trying to take down a forest?" he asks, his tone half-teasing, half-serious.

I shrug, focusing on the pile of wood at my feet. "Just needed to get some work done."

Sam's quiet for a moment, and I can almost hear the gears turning in his head. Finally, he sighs, crossing his arms over his chest. "Look, Jack, I'm not gonna dance around this. You've been on your own for a long time, and I get why. But you've got something good here with Natalie. Don't screw it up because you're too scared to let her in."

His words hit me harder than I want to admit. Sam's always been the one to call me out, to push me when I needed it, but this feels different. It feels like he's holding up a mirror, forcing me to see the truth I've been trying to avoid.

"It's not that simple," I say, my voice rougher than I intended.

"Maybe not," Sam agrees, his tone softening. "But nothing worth having ever is."

I glance at him, seeing the concern in his eyes, the way he's rooting for me, even when I'm not sure I deserve it. "I don't know if I can do it, Sam. Letting someone in... it's risky."

"It is," he says, nodding. "But so is living your life alone, never taking a chance on something real. You've been alone long enough, Jack. Maybe it's time to take that risk."

His words hang in the air between us, heavy with meaning. I want to argue, to push back, to retreat into the safety of my solitude. But there's a part of me—a part I've been trying to ignore—that knows he's right. That knows I've been running from life, not living it.

Sam claps me on the shoulder, his grip firm and reassuring. "Think about it," he says, before turning and heading back through the snow toward his truck.

I watch him go, the weight of his words settling over me like a fresh blanket of snow. The peace I felt when I woke up is gone, replaced by a gnawing uncertainty. I don't know what to do, don't know if I'm ready to let Natalie in, to risk my heart again. But as I stand there, the cold biting at my skin, I know one thing for sure: I can't keep running forever.

I glance back toward the cabin, where I know Natalie is still inside, probably wondering why I've been avoiding her all morning. My heart clenches at the thought of her, the way she looked last night, the way she trusted me with her fears. She's not just someone passing through—she's become important to me, in a way I didn't see coming.

And that scares me more than anything.

But maybe, just maybe, it's time to stop letting fear control me. Maybe it's time to let someone in.

CHAPTER 9

Natalie

THE MORNING SUN streams through the cabin windows, casting a warm golden glow over the entire room. The light dances gently across the wooden surfaces, illuminating the dust motes that swirl lazily in the air. Outside, the snow that had blanketed the world just hours ago is beginning to melt, the pristine white landscape slowly giving way to patches of brown earth and glistening puddles that reflect the sunlight like tiny mirrors. It's a tranquil scene, one that should fill me with a profound sense of calm and serenity, but my mind is anything but quiet. Instead, thoughts race through my head, tumultuous and chaotic, drowning out the peaceful beauty that surrounds me.

I drive back to the Buttercup Inn when Jack is nowhere to be found. As I'm standing by the window, watching the sunlight dance on the snow, my phone buzzes on the table. The sharp, insistent vibration cuts through the warmth of the cabin, pulling me back to a reality I've been avoiding since I arrived in Buttercup Bay. I glance at the screen and see my boss's name flashing. My heart sinks, and with it, the tranquility of the morning.

"Hello?" I answer, my voice more uncertain than I'd like.

"Natalie, it's Janine. Just checking in on your progress with the campaign. We've got deadlines coming up, and we need to make sure everything is on track," she says, her tone brisk and businesslike, as if the world outside her office hasn't changed at all.

The sound of her voice is like a splash of cold water, jolting me back to reality, a stark reminder of the life I left behind in the bustling city. I can almost picture her sitting at her desk, surrounded by towering stacks of paperwork and the incessant hum of office chatter, completely disconnected from the serene, quiet beauty that envelops me here in Buttercup Bay. The contrast is striking, and I feel a pang of guilt wash over me, knowing that my mind has been far from the deadlines she's worried about, drifting instead in the idyllic stillness of this moment.

"Of course," I say, forcing myself to focus. "Everything's on track. I'll have the final draft ready by the end of the week."

"Good. We're counting on you, Natalie. This campaign is important," Janine replies, her voice cutting through any remnants of the peace I felt this morning.

"I understand," I manage, but the words feel hollow.

The call ends as abruptly as it began, leaving me standing in the middle of the Buttercup Inn, my phone still clutched in my hand. The room is warm, the fire crackling softly in the hearth, but I feel a chill creeping into my bones. The reality of the situation is settling over me like a heavy blanket—I'm torn between two worlds, and I have to choose.

I set the phone down and turn back to the window, my eyes tracing the lines of the snow-covered trees as they begin to glisten in the morning sun. Buttercup Bay has awakened something in me, something I didn't even know I was missing. There's a longing in my chest, a yearning for connection and belonging that I've never felt in the city. But that longing comes with a cost—if I give in to it, I'm risking everything I've worked so hard to achieve.

The career I've built, the independence I've fought for—it all seems so far away now, yet it's a part of who I am. The city is where I've proven myself, where I've shown that I can succeed on my own. But standing here, in this quiet cabin surrounded by nature, with the memory of last night's kiss still lingering on my lips, I'm starting to wonder if that's enough.

The sound of the inn's front door opening startles me, and I turn to see Maggie stepping inside, brushing the melting snow off her boots. Her eyes find mine immediately, and I know she's here because she senses my turmoil.

"Natalie," she says warmly, her voice a balm to my frayed nerves. "I was hoping I'd find you here."

"Maggie," I reply, trying to smile, but I can't quite manage it. "I was just... thinking."

"I can see that," she says gently, her gaze soft but knowing. "Why don't you come down to the café with me? I've got a fresh apple pie that's just begging to be shared."

The thought of stepping out of the inn, out of this space where everything feels so uncertain, is both a relief and a challenge. But I nod, knowing that I could use the distraction.

The walk to the café is quiet, the snow crunching softly under our boots as we make our way down the path. The town is just starting to wake up, the sun reflecting off the wet rooftops and casting long shadows across the street. It's a scene that feels both familiar and foreign, a place that's starting to feel like home but still holds so much uncertainty.

When we step into the warmth of the café, the smell of fresh-baked pie envelops me, comforting and nostalgic. Maggie leads me to a small table near the window, where the sun streams in, casting a soft light over the worn wood. She brings over two slices of warm apple pie, the steam rising from the golden crust, and sits across from me, her expression kind and patient.

"Tell me what's on your mind," Maggie says, her voice gentle but firm, like she already knows the weight of the decision I'm carrying.

I take a deep breath, the scent of cinnamon and apples filling my lungs, and try to find the words. "I got a call from my boss this morning," I begin, my voice quiet. "It reminded me of everything I've been trying to forget since I got here—the deadlines, the career I've built, the life I've fought so hard for. And now... now I'm not sure if I can go back to that."

Maggie nods, her eyes full of understanding. "Buttercup Bay has a way of doing that," she says softly. "It makes you question what really matters."

I look down at the pie in front of me, the golden crust and the sweet filling that should be comforting, but all I feel is the weight of the decision pressing down on me. "I've spent so much of my life trying to prove that I could make it on my own," I say, my voice trembling. "But being here, with Jack, with all of you... it's made me realize how lonely that life has been."

Maggie reaches across the table, taking my hand in hers. Her touch is warm, grounding me in the moment. "You're not alone anymore, Natalie," she says gently. "But I understand the fear. I've been there."

I look up, surprised by the emotion in her voice. "You have?"

Maggie smiles, a sad, wistful smile that reflects a past filled with its own share of heartache and longing. "I had a love once," she begins, her voice soft, almost as if she is afraid to disturb the delicate memories. "His name was Henry. We met here, in Buttercup Bay, a place that once felt like the center of our universe, and for a while, it truly felt like the world was ours to explore together. But life has a way of testing us, and we were no exception to that rule. He had dreams that took him far from this beautiful coastal town, while I had roots that kept me firmly grounded in the life I had built here. We tried our best to make it work, pouring our hearts into late-night conversations and hopeful promises, but in the end, we found ourselves at a crossroads, and we had to let each other go."

I listen, captivated by the quiet strength in her words, the way she speaks of love and loss with such grace. "But you stayed," I say, trying to understand how she found the strength to keep going.

Maggie nods, her eyes misty with the memories she's sharing. "I stayed because Buttercup Bay is my home. It's where I found myself again, where I learned that love isn't about holding on too tight but about letting go when it's right. And it's where I learned that taking a risk for love is worth it, even if it means facing the unknown."

Her words resonate deep within me, touching the part of my heart that's been aching for something more, something real. I think of Jack, of the way he looked at me last night, the way he made me feel seen, understood, and cherished in a way I've never experienced before. The idea of leaving him, of walking away from this connection we've started to build, feels unbearable.

But the fear is still there, too—fear of giving up the life I've known, of stepping into the unknown, of risking everything for something that might not last. And yet, as I sit here, the warmth of the café surrounding me, Maggie's words echo in my mind: taking a risk for love is worth it.

I squeeze Maggie's hand, a surge of gratitude swelling in my chest. "Thank you," I whisper, my voice thick with emotion. "I needed to hear that."

Maggie smiles, a knowing glint in her eyes. "You're welcome, dear. Just remember, whatever decision you make, it's your life to live. But don't be afraid to follow your heart. Sometimes, it knows the way better than your head does."

As we finish our pie, the decision I've been avoiding starts to take shape in my mind. It's not an easy choice, and it's one that will change everything, but as I sit here, surrounded by the warmth of Buttercup Bay and the memory of Jack's kiss, I know that I can't go back to the way things were. My heart has found something here, something worth fighting for, and maybe it's time to take that risk.

The sun outside is brighter now, casting a golden glow that dances across the landscape, the snow melting away to reveal the vibrant earth beneath. I can't help but feel like I'm standing on the edge of a new beginning, a thrilling precipice teetering between anticipation and fear. It's terrifying, yet exhilarating, a rush of possibilities flooding my senses. As I step out of the café, the crisp air fills my lungs, invigorating me, and I know that whatever happens next, I'm ready to face it with newfound courage.

CHAPTER 10

Jack

THE CABIN IS enveloped in a profound quiet, too quiet. It's the unsettling kind of quiet that allows doubts and fears to creep in, insidiously filling the silence with thoughts I desperately don't want to confront. I've been laboring on the roof all morning, methodically repairing the damage wrought by the recent storm, but no matter how hard I focus on the task at hand, trying to lose myself in the rhythm of the work, I can't shake the deep emptiness that has settled uncomfortably in my chest, like a weight that refuses to budge.

It doesn't feel like home without Natalie here.

I lean against the ladder, wiping the sweat from my brow despite the cool autumn air. The sun is bright, reflecting off the patches of snow that still cling to the ground, but it does little to warm the cold knot of fear that's been sitting in my stomach since she left this morning. Fear that I've already lost her. Fear that I'm not strong enough to hold on.

Sam's words echo in my mind, pushing at the edges of my resolve. *You've been alone long enough, Jack. Maybe it's time to take that risk.* I didn't want to hear it then, but now, with the emptiness of the cabin pressing in on me, I can't ignore it.

I've spent so long convincing myself that solitude was safer, that keeping my distance was the only way to protect myself from the pain of losing someone I care about. But all it's done is keep me isolated, locked away from the very things I've started to realize I want. The things I need.

And what I need now is Natalie.

I take a deep breath, the air cold and sharp in my lungs, filling me with a clarity I hadn't felt in a long time. I push away from the ladder, the rough wood pressing against my palms as I release my grip. The repairs can wait; they'll still be there later, a reminder of the work that needs to be done. But right now, there's something more important I need to do. Something that can't wait another minute—something that has been simmering beneath the surface for far too long.

The decision settles over me with a strange sense of calm. For the first time in a long time, I know what I want, and I'm done letting fear stand in my way. I grab my jacket and keys, my heart pounding as I step out into the crisp autumn afternoon.

The drive to Buttercup Bay feels longer than usual, each mile stretching out before me like an eternity as I mentally rehearse the words I'm going to say to Natalie. They dance just out of reach, elusive and reluctant, and the truth is, they never have come easily to me. But deep down, I know I need to find the courage to tell her how I truly feel. She deserves to know that I'm ready to fight for her, for us, even if it means stepping out of the comforting safety of the life I've painstakingly built around myself. The thought of that life, with its familiar routines and predictable boundaries, both reassures and terrifies me, yet I can't ignore the undeniable truth that some things are worth the risk.

The town is alive with the energy of the Halloween Bash when I arrive, the square filled with the sounds of laughter and music. The decorations are up, vibrant and festive, with twinkling lights strung across the buildings and pumpkins lining the sidewalks. There's a chill in the air, but it's offset by the warmth of the crowd, the sense of community that I've always kept at arm's length.

Until now.

I park the truck and step out, the lively atmosphere enveloping me as I make my way through the throng of people. My heart hammers in my chest, a relentless rhythm echoing my nervous anticipation as I scan the faces around me, searching for Natalie. The lights above twinkle like stars, casting a warm and inviting glow over the vibrant scene, illuminating the laughter and joy that fills the air. Yet, despite the festive spirit surrounding me, all I can focus on is finding her, the urgency of sharing the words I should have said days ago weighing heavily on my mind.

And then I see her.

She's standing near the center of the square, talking with Maggie and a few other townsfolk, her smile soft and genuine. The sight of her takes my breath away, and for a moment, I just stand there, watching her, letting the reality of what I'm about to do sink in.

This is it. No more running. No more hiding.

I take a deep breath, steadying myself as I step forward, weaving through the bustling crowd that laughs and chats, the warmth of their joy wrapping around me like a comforting blanket. Each step feels like a small victory, a defiance against the fears that have held me back for too long, until I'm finally standing right in front of her. The moment she looks up and locks her gaze with mine, her smile falters, replaced by a mix of surprise and something else—something that looks like hope, flickering in her eyes like the soft glow of lantern light on a chilly evening.

"Natalie," I say, my voice rough with emotion. The crowd around us seems to fade, the music and laughter dimming as I focus on the only thing that matters right now. "I need to tell you something."

She looks up at me, her eyes wide, and I can see the questions swirling there, the uncertainty that mirrors my own. But there's no turning back now.

"I've spent a long time thinking that it was safer to be alone," I begin, the words coming out slowly, each one heavy with meaning. "That if I kept people at a distance, I wouldn't get hurt. And it worked, for a while. But then you came along, and suddenly, all that solitude didn't feel like safety anymore. It felt like a prison."

Her eyes soften, and she takes a small step closer, her breath visible in the cool night air. "Jack..."

"I'm not good at this," I admit, my voice breaking slightly. "But I need you to know that I don't want to be alone anymore. Not if it means losing you. I'm ready to take that risk, to fight for what we have, if you're willing to do the same."

The crowd around us has quieted, the energy shifting like a tide as people begin to realize something significant is unfolding. Whispers fade into silence, and the atmosphere thickens with anticipation. I can feel the weight of their eyes on us, a thousand curious gazes probing for a glimpse of what's to come, but I don't care. Their intrigue, their judgment—it all fades into the background. All that matters is Natalie, standing just a breath away, her presence illuminating the moment like a beacon in the night.

"I'm falling for you, Natalie," I say, the words finally spilling out, raw and honest. "I want a future with you. Whatever that looks like, wherever it takes us, I want to face it together. I'm done running. I'm done hiding. I'm here, and I'm ready if you are."

For a moment, the world seems to stop, the air thick with anticipation as I wait for her response. My heart is pounding so hard I can barely hear anything else, and the fear is there, clawing at my chest, but it's overshadowed by the need to know what she's going to say.

And then she smiles.

It's a smile that lights up her whole face, radiating warmth and joy, a brilliance that reaches her eyes and melts away every doubt I've been carrying like a heavy weight on my shoulders. She steps closer, closing the distance between us with an ease that feels both exhilarating and terrifying, and I can see the tears glistening in her eyes, shimmering like tiny stars in the night sky, though they're beautifully matched by the brightness of her smile, a beacon of hope that fills my heart with a rush of emotions I can hardly contain.

"I'm falling for you too, Jack," she says, her voice trembling with emotion. "I've been so afraid of what it would mean to stay here, to build a life with you. But I don't want to run either. I want to face whatever comes, as long as we're together."

The relief that floods through me is overwhelming, a wave of emotion that nearly knocks me off my feet. I pull her into my arms, holding her close as the crowd around us erupts in cheers and applause, but all I can focus on is the feel of her against me, the warmth of her body, the way she fits so perfectly in my arms.

The lights above us twinkle like stars, and for the first time in years, I feel like I'm exactly where I'm supposed to be.

We kiss, and it's everything—tender and passionate, infused with all the emotions we've been holding back for far too long. It's a moment that feels both electrifying and serene, a perfect blend of longing and relief. The world around us fades away, dissolving into a blur of sounds and colors, leaving only the two of us, entwined in each other's arms. Together.

CHAPTER 11

Natalie

HE LOVES ME. Jack Wilder, the man who's spent so long guarding his heart, just stood in front of the entire town and confessed his love for me. And in that instant, everything I've been struggling with—the doubts, the fears, the questions—falls away, leaving only one truth behind.

This is what I've been searching for all along. Not a career that would define my worth, not a title that would elevate my status, not a place in the bustling city that would drown me in its chaos, but this. A love that envelops me and makes me feel truly alive, a connection that ignites a warmth in my heart and makes me feel like I finally belong in this world.

The realization is overwhelming, filling every part of me with a warmth that's almost too much to bear. I feel the tears welling up in my eyes, but they're not from sadness—they're from the sheer relief and joy that comes with knowing I've found something real, something worth fighting for.

Jack is standing there, his eyes locked on mine, waiting for me to say something, anything. I can see the nervousness in the way his hands clench at his sides, the way his chest rises and falls with each breath. He's put everything on the line, and now it's my turn.

I take a step forward, closing the distance between us. My heart is racing, my hands trembling as I reach up to cup his face, feeling the roughness of his stubble against my palms. The warmth of his skin seeps into me, grounding me in this moment, making everything else fall away.

The words spill out of me, raw and honest, carrying with them all the emotions I've been holding back. "I've been so scared of what it would mean to stay here, to give up everything I've worked for. But none of it matters—not without you. You make me feel alive, you make me feel like I belong. And I don't want to lose that. I don't want to lose you."

His eyes soften, and I see the relief flood through him, washing away the tension that's been holding him rigid. He pulls me closer, his arms wrapping around me, and I feel the strength of his embrace, the way he's holding on to me like he never wants to let go.

The town around us seems to fade away, the sounds of the festival dimming until there's only the two of us, standing together under the twinkling lights. I can see the stars reflected in his eyes, the soft glow of the lanterns casting a warm light over his face, and in that moment, everything feels right. Like this is exactly where I'm supposed to be.

And then he kisses me.

It's a kiss that's both tender and passionate, infused with all the love and longing we've been holding back for what feels like an eternity. His lips are warm against mine, sending a delightful shiver through me, the feel of him so familiar yet exhilaratingly new, as if we're embarking on a journey of discovery together all over again. I lose myself completely in the kiss, surrendering to the way he holds me so securely, the way he makes me feel like I'm the only person in the world, cherished and adored in this perfect moment that seems to stretch on forever.

When we finally pull apart, we're both breathless, our foreheads resting together as we try to steady ourselves, sharing an intimate moment that feels suspended in time. I can hear the vibrant sound of the festival around us once more—the laughter of children playing, the lively music weaving through the air, and the distant clatter of dishes being served—but it all feels strangely distant, as if it's happening in another world entirely, a mere backdrop to the magic we've just created together.

"Natalie," Jack whispers, his voice rough with emotion. "You're my home."

The words hit me like a bolt of lightning, striking straight to my heart. I smile, tears spilling over as I realize that he's right. He's my home too. He's the place where I belong.

"I love you," I say again, my voice stronger this time, filled with certainty. "And I'm not going anywhere."

The world around us slowly comes back into focus, and I realize that we're not alone. The townsfolk are watching us, their faces lit with smiles, their eyes bright with shared joy. Maggie and Sam are standing together, exchanging knowing smiles, and I see Maggie wipe a tear from her eye as she nods in our direction, a silent show of support.

The crowd starts to cheer, the sound filling the square with warmth and celebration. The sense of community, of belonging, is palpable, wrapping around us like a comforting embrace. I've never felt anything like it, this feeling of being accepted, of being part of something bigger than myself.

Jack pulls me close again, his arm wrapped securely around my waist, and I lean into him, finding comfort as I rest my head against his warm chest. I can feel his heartbeat, strong and steady, echoing the rhythm of my own, a reassuring reminder of our shared experience. The steady thump resonates in the stillness around us, and in that intimate moment, I know that everything we've been through—the trials, the laughter, the tears—has led us to this: a profound moment of love, of deep connection, and of true belonging.

The lights above us twinkle like stars, and as I look up at them, I feel a sense of peace settle over me. This is where I'm meant to be, with Jack, in this town that has welcomed me with open arms. I've found my place, my home, and it's not in a city skyscraper or a corner office. It's here, in Buttercup Bay, with the man I love and the people who have become my family.

The festival continues around us, the music picking up again as people return to their celebrations, but I stay there, wrapped in Jack's arms, savoring the moment. The future is still uncertain, but for the first time in my life, I'm not afraid of what comes next.

Because I know, without a doubt, that whatever happens, we'll face it together.

CHAPTER 12

Epilogue

THE CABIN IS FILLED with the scent of freshly baked bread, its warmth mingling with the crisp, pine-scented breeze that drifts in through the open windows. Outside, Buttercup Bay is alive with the promise of spring—trees adorned with fresh green leaves, flowers in full bloom, and the sunlight streaming down in golden rays. It's the kind of morning that fills you with a sense of renewal, of new beginnings, and I can't help but smile as I take it all in.

It's hard to believe how much has changed in just a few months. This cabin, once just a shelter, has become our home—a place filled with love, laughter, and the quiet comfort of shared moments. The walls are decorated with little pieces of our life together photos of the festival where Jack first confessed his love, a collection of books we've started reading to each other in the evenings, and the quilt Maggie made for us as a housewarming gift. Each item tells a story, a reminder of the journey we've taken to get here.

As I pull the golden-brown loaf of bread from the oven, the irresistible smell of warm, yeasty goodness fills the kitchen, wrapping around me like a comforting embrace. I watch as steam rises gently from the crust, and I can't help but smile at the sight. In this moment, a profound sense of contentment settles over me, enveloping my heart in a cozy warmth. This is what I was searching for all along—not a career filled with accolades, not a title that carries weight, but a place where I truly belong, surrounded by the laughter and love of someone who makes me feel vibrantly alive. The simple act of baking transforms into a celebration of togetherness, a reminder that happiness is found in these small, shared moments.

"Smells amazing," Jack says as he steps into the kitchen, his voice filled with that familiar warmth that never fails to make my heart flutter. He leans in to kiss my cheek, his hand resting on the small of my back as he does. "I could get used to this."

I laugh, nudging him playfully. "You already have."

He grins, his eyes crinkling at the corners in that charming way that always makes me smile in return, and I can't help but marvel at how easy everything feels now—how natural it is to be here with him, immersed in the warmth of his presence, sharing these simple, everyday moments that mean so much. The way his laughter dances in the air and the light in his gaze makes everything else fade away, leaving just us in this cozy sanctuary of familiarity and joy.

Before I can respond, there's a knock at the door, followed by Maggie's cheerful voice. "I hope you two are hungry! I've brought enough produce to feed an army."

Jack and I exchange amused glances before heading to the door together. Maggie stands there, holding a basket overflowing with fresh vegetables and herbs, her face lit up with the joy that always seems to radiate from her.

"Come on in, Maggie," I say, stepping aside to let

her in. "The bread just came out of the oven, so you're right on time."

She beams at me, her eyes twinkling. "Perfect timing, as always."

As Maggie sets the basket on the counter, the door opens again, and Sam steps inside, wiping his hands on a rag. "Got those repairs finished up," he says, nodding to Jack. "This place will be ready in no time."

"Thanks, Sam," Jack replies, clapping him on the back. "Couldn't have done it without you."

The four of us move to the table, where I've already set out plates and silverware. The smell of the freshly baked bread mixes with the earthy scent of the produce Maggie brought, and I can't help but feel a surge of gratitude for these people, this place, this life.

As we settle down at the table to enjoy our meal, the conversation flows effortlessly, punctuated by laughter and animated stories about the upcoming summer festival that everyone is so eagerly anticipating. The sound of our voices fills the cozy cabin, echoing off the wooden walls that have witnessed so much change in such a short span of time. There's a palpable warmth here, a deep sense of community that I've never experienced before, and it wraps around me like a comforting embrace, making me feel as if I truly belong. Each shared moment and playful exchange binds us closer together, reinforcing the bonds of friendship and camaraderie that make this gathering so special.

I glance over at Jack, who's deep in conversation with Sam about the best way to set up the booths for the festival. There's a lightness in his expression, a joy that I know wasn't there before, and it makes my heart swell with love for him. This is what we've built together—a life filled with love, support, and the promise of a future that we're both excited to face.

After the meal, Maggie and Sam head out, leaving Jack and me alone in the quiet of the afternoon. The sun is beginning to dip lower in the sky, casting long shadows across the porch as we step outside. The air is still, the only sound the distant call of a bird as it flies overhead.

We sit together on the porch swing, the weathered wood creaking softly under our weight as we settle in, finding comfort in the gentle sway. Jack wraps an arm around my shoulders, pulling me close, and I rest my head against his chest, feeling the warmth radiate from him as I listen to the steady, rhythmic beat of his heart. The sunset paints the mountains in breathtaking hues of orange and pink, the colors so vibrant and alive it's almost as if the sky itself is ablaze, igniting the world around us in a stunning display of nature's artistry. Each moment feels precious, wrapped in the tranquility of the evening, a reminder of the beauty that surrounds us.

"I never thought I'd find this," I say quietly, my voice filled with wonder. "A place where I truly belong."

Jack tilts his head to look down at me, his expression tender. "You've always belonged here, Natalie. It just took a little time to find your way."

I smile, closing my eyes as I soak in the warmth of his words, the truth in them settling deep in my heart. "I'm so glad I did."

We sit there in comfortable silence, watching as the sky changes colors, the day slowly giving way to night. The stars begin to peek out, one by one, until the sky is filled with them, twinkling like tiny diamonds against the velvet backdrop.

As the last of the daylight fades, Jack takes my hand in his, his fingers lacing through mine. "Whatever comes next, we'll face it together," he says, his voice steady and sure.

I nod, feeling a sense of peace wash over me. "Together," I agree, knowing that there's no place I'd rather be than right here, with him, ready to take on whatever the future holds.

The night air is cool, but I don't feel the chill. All I feel is the warmth of Jack beside me, the steady beat of his heart, and the deep, abiding love that we share. This is my home, my future, my new beginning.

And as we sit there, hand in hand, watching the stars above us, I know that we're exactly where we're meant to be.

Leave a review!

If you enjoyed this book, take a moment to leave a review. This allows your fellow readers to determine if this is a good book for them.

Thank you!

www.ingramcontent.com/pod-product-compliance
Lightning Source LLC
Chambersburg PA
CBHW031740150726
47989CB00006B/2544